Arnie and His School Tools

Arnie and His School Tools

Simple Sensory Solutions
That Build Success

Jennifer Veenendall

©2008 Autism Asperger Publishing Company
P.O. Box 23173
Shawnee Mission, Kansas 66283-0173
www.asperger.net

Publisher's Cataloging-in-Publication

Veenendall, Jennifer.

    Arnie and his school tools : simple sensory solutions that build success / Jennifer Veenendall. -- 1st ed. -- Shawnee Mission, Kan. : Autism Asperger Pub. Co., 2008.

       p. ; cm.

    ISBN: 978-1-934575-15-4
    LCCN: 2007939600
    Includes a brief overview of sensory processing as well as discussion questions.
    Includes bibliographical references.
    Summary: Arnie uses a variety of tools and materials that provide his nervous system with the additional movement, touch, oral, and heavy work input that he needs to be more successful. He also uses tools to limit sound because he is very sensitive to auditory distractions.

    1. Children with disabilities--Education. 2. Sensory integration dysfunction in children. 3. Sensorimotor integration. 4. Occupational therapy for children. 5. Children with disabilities--Juvenile fiction. I. Title. II. Simple sensory solutions that build success.

RJ496 .S44 V44 2008
618.928--dc22   0712

This book is designed in CG Benguiat Frisky.

Printed in the United States of America.

To all of my "Arnies," who have taught me so much.

Acknowledgments

I would like to thank Mary Sue Williams and Shelly Shellenberger for their *How Does Your Engine Run? Alert Program for Self-Regulation.* They have provided occupational therapists, teachers, and families with a brilliant tool to help children with sensory modulation difficulties feel more understood and confident, and more in control of their success at home and at school. This book is intended to be used with such a program to help all elementary students understand the basic concepts of sensory modulation and tools that may be used by all of us to "tune our engines," when necessary.

Hi! I'm Arnie. I didn't use to like school very much.

But now I do, and I want to tell you why.

School used to be hard. Really hard!
That was before I learned about my School Tools.

I'm a lot like my friends. I like to play video games and draw pictures.
I especially like to draw dinosaurs.

At school my favorite class is gym. I'm a pretty good basketball player.
I just lost my fourth tooth; most of my friends have only lost two or three.

I'm different from a lot of my friends in another way, too.
I'm a MOVER. My motor runs a little higher than most other kids'.
That means it's harder for me to sit still and pay attention.

Some kids can sit on their pockets on their carpet spot, listen to Mrs. Reinke give directions for our writing assignment, and then go back to their desks and finish their work without ANY reminders.

Not me! I can't sit in one place for very long. My body needs to move. My hands need to be busy. I have a hard time listening only to my teacher. I used to find things on the floor or on the wall to touch and play with. Sometimes I would play with my shoelaces or touch other kids. My teacher used to say, "Arnie! Keep your hands to yourself, please." "Arnie! Sit still." Or "Arnie! Pay attention."

I wanted to listen to my teachers, but it's hard   to listen to their directions when all I can hear is Mr. Brown's class playing "Buzz" next door.

Just like a construction worker needs tools to build a house, I need tools to get my work done. I don't need hammers or circular saws, or those kinds of tools. I need "Tools for Learning."

When it's hard for me to sit still in my desk, sometimes I use a special cushion in my seat that lets me move around a little. Sometimes I sit on a big ball instead of a chair. Once in a while I stand to do my work. My teachers say that's okay.

During listening times, I hold a "fidget." At first, my friends thought it was a toy, but now they know it's a tool to help me focus. It's a hand tool.

I also have tools that I use with my mouth. I have a special piece of
plastic on my pencil that I chew on. Sometimes I use crunchy or chewy
food to help me concentrate.

I have a heavy blanket I use on my lap sometimes.
Or I wear a heavy vest. It feels a little like I'm getting a hug, and it
helps me relax so I can do my work better.

When I'm listening to Mr. Brown's class next door instead of focusing on my writing journal in the morning, I can wear headphones or earplugs. That helps me tune out the sounds around me that distract me from doing my work.

When I really need to move, like during a long calendar time, Mrs. Reinke might ask me to run an errand for her to the office or another teacher's room. I also help her pass out supplies and papers.

Sometimes my teacher has the whole class get up
and do exercises or stretches to music.

Certain times at school are extra hard for me. For example, I always bring a fidget to assemblies because it is difficult for me to sit on the gym floor for a long time.

Recess is easy! I love to run and jump and climb and swing. But coming back inside is not always so easy.

That's when I have what we call my "job time." Mr. Dave is our custodian, and I am his special helper. Sometimes I help him sweep the cafeteria floor. I also push a heavy cart to deliver boxes of mail to teachers. Then when I go back to my class, my motor isn't running too high any more, and I am ready to concentrate and do my work.

I work very hard at school to keep my body as calm as I can so I feel better and learn better. When I get home, my mom lets me play before I sit down to do my homework.

I have my very own homework desk in our office at home. It is a quiet place, so I don't need earplugs. I sit on a ball chair when I work, and I take a short break every 10 minutes. While I'm working, I eat food to help me concentrate, like chewy dried fruit or crunchy pretzels. I drink water from my water bottle with a straw.

Sometimes I jump on our mini-trampoline, and at other times I jump and crash into our couch pillows.

All these things help calm my body and my mind so I can get my homework done.

My teachers help me figure out what tools work the best for me, and I'm always learning about new tools. My teachers talk to my mom and dad about things we can try at home, too. Sometimes I try tools that don't work well for me. When that happens, we just cross them off my list and try something else.

Arnie's School Tools

When my motor is running too high, I can use these tools to help me.
1. ball chair
2. chewy
3. vest
4. fidget
5. exercises
6. headphones

Yesterday I learned that I can kick a stretchy band tied to the legs of my chair when my legs feel like moving but my brain wants me to sit down and finish my "M Is for Monkey" art project.

It might always be harder for me to do things that I need to sit down and concentrate on, but my School Tools are helping me.

My mom says that when I grow up I probably won't be an accountant
like my dad, because he has to sit at a desk most of the day.
Instead, maybe I'll be an archeologist and discover the bones of a
dinosaur no one knew about. I already know a lot about dinosaurs!

Sensory Processing and Sensory Modulation Disorders

Carol Stock Kranowitz describes sensory processing disorder in her book *The Out-of-Sync Child* (2005) as "the inability to use information received through the senses in order to function smoothly in daily life" (p. 9). There are different types of sensory processing disorders. Arnie in this book is an example of somebody who has difficulties with a type of sensory processing disorder called sensory modulation. His nervous system has a hard time responding to some sensory stimuli and ignoring others so he can respond appropriately to everyday situations that most of us pay little attention to. For example, it is difficult for him to achieve a "just right" state where he feels calm but is also alert and ready to learn. With the help of his teachers, parents, and occupational therapist, he has learned to use sensorimotor strategies to help him self-regulate.

Occupational therapists often work with individuals with sensory processing disorders. In addition to occupational therapy with a sensory integration focus, children with sensory modulation difficulties benefit from adaptations in their environment to accommodate for their sensory processing pattern. Also, sensorimotor activities help them maintain an optimal level of alertness for daily functional tasks.

Arnie uses a variety of tools and materials that provide his nervous system with the additional movement, touch, oral and heavy work input that he needs to be more successful. He also uses tools to limit sound because he is very sensitive to auditory distractions.

Suggested Discussion Questions Following Reading the Book with a Child or a Group of Children

1. **What does it feel like to have a high engine or motor?** (You have a hard time focusing. You might feel really excited, nervous, or even angry. It is hard to sit still. Discuss when it is OK to have a high engine. Maybe outside at recess time, when you are cheering at a soccer game, when you are riding a rollercoaster, etc.)

2. **What does it mean to have a motor that is running too low?** (You have a hard time focusing. You might feel tired or bored; your parents may call you lazy. Your teacher might think you are daydreaming. Talk about when it is OK to have a low engine, such as when you are feeling sick or when you are trying to fall asleep at night.)

3. **What does it mean to have a "just right" engine?** (You can listen, follow directions, and get work done. You feel happy and proud, and your body is calm.)

4. **What are some of Arnie's School Tools that he used to help him keep his body calm so he can focus on his schoolwork?** (fidget, pencil chewy, crunchy or chewy food, ear protectors/plugs, weighted vest, weighted blanket, ball chair, seat cushion, stretchy chair leg band)

5. **Arnie uses tools to help him when his engine runs too high or too low. Think about other types of tools people might use to help them be more successful.**
   - What tool would a person use if she could not see as well as others? (glasses)
   - What would a person use if he could not hear as much as others? (hearing aid)
   - How about a student whose muscles work differently and has a hard time walking? (walker or wheelchair)

Recommended Resources for Teachers and Parents

Aquilla, P., Sutton, S., & Yack, E. (2002). *Building bridges through sensory integration*. Las Vegas, NV: Sensory Resources.

Biel, L., & Peske, N. K. (2005). *Raising a sensory smart child*. New York: Penguin Books.

Brack, J. (2004). *Learn to move, move to learn: Sensorimotor early childhood activity themes*. Shawnee Mission, KS: Autism Asperger Publishing Company.

Brack, J. (2005). *Sensory processing disorder: Simulations & solutions for parents, teachers and therapists* (DVD). Shawnee Mission, KS: Autism Asperger Publishing Company.

Cermack, S., Koomar, J., Silver, D., & Szklut, S. (1998). *Making sense of sensory integration* [Audiocassette and booklet]. Boulder, CO: Bell Curve Records.

Davalos, S. R. (2000). *Making sense of art: Sensory-based activities for children with autism, Asperger Syndrome and other pervasive developmental disorders*. Shawnee Mission, KS: Autism Asperger Publishing Company.

Frick, S., Oetter, P., & Richter, E. (1995). *M.O.R.E.: Integrating the mouth with sensory and postural functions* (2nd ed.). Hugo, MN: PDP Press.

Fuge, G., & Berry, R. (2004). *Pathways to play! Combining sensory integration and integrated play groups.* Shawnee Mission, KS: Autism Asperger Publishing Company.

Godwin Emmans, P., & McEndry Anderson, L. (2005). *Understanding sensory dysfunction: Learning, development and sensory dysfunction in autism spectrum disorders, ADHD, learning disabilities and bipolar disorder*. London; Philadelphia: Jessica Kingsley Publishers.

Henry, D. A. (2000). *Toolchest for teachers, parents, and students: A handbook to facilitate self-regulation*. Phoenix, AZ: Henry Occupational Therapy Service, Inc.

Koomar, J., Kranowitz, C., & Szklut, S. Balzer-Martin, L., Haber, E., & Sava, D., (2004). *Answers to questions teachers ask about sensory integration*. Las Vegas, NV: Sensory Resources LLC.

Kranowitz, C. (1995). *101 activities for kids in tight spaces*. New York: St. Martin's.

Kranowitz, C. (2005). *The out-of-sync child: Recognizing and coping with sensory processing disorder, 2nd edition*. New York: Perigee Books. Kranowitz, C. (2006). *The out-out-sync child has fun: Activities for kids with sensory processing disorder, 2nd edition*. New York: Perigee Books.

Miller, L. (2006). *Sensational kids*. New York: G. P. Putnam's Sons.

Myles, B. S., Cook, K. T., Miller. N. E., Rinner, L., & Robbins, L. A. (2000). *Asperger syndrome and sensory issues: Practical solutions for making sense of the world*. Shawnee Mission, KS: Autism Asperger Publishing Company.

Patton, S. (2008). *Take a break with the sensory gang*. Shawnee Mission, KS: Autism Asperger Publishing Company.

Sangirardi Ganz, J. (2005). *Including SI for parents: Sensory integration strategies at home and school*. Prospect, CT: Biographical Publishing Company.

Shellenberger, S., & Williams, M. S. (1994). *An introduction to how does your engine run?: The alert program for self-regulation*. Albuquerque, NM: Therapy Works, Inc.

Shellenberger, S., & Williams, M. S. (1996). *How does your engine run?: A leader's guide to the alert program for self-regulation*. Albuquerque, NM: Therapy Works, Inc.

Shellenberger, S., & Williams, M. S. (2001). *Take five! Staying alert at home and school*. Albuquerque, NM: Therapy Works, Inc.

Useful Websites

1. www.alertprogram.com
   This is the Alert Program (Shellenberger & Williams) website. It describes the program and offers products, conference information, articles, and other resources related to the Alert Program.

2. www.henryot.com
   This is the Henry Occupational Therapy Services, Inc. site. It includes a variety of products useful to parents, teachers, and students written by Diane A. Henry. It also provides information about workshops, articles, and other resources related to sensory processing disorders.

3. www.SensoryResources.com
   The Sensory Resources website specializes in sensory issues. It offers products such as books, CDs, videos, and DVDs as well as information on workshops and conferences.

4. www.sensorysmarts.com
   This is the website by the authors of *Raising a Sensory Smart Child* (Biel & Peske, 2005). It includes several useful sections with tips and resources for parents of children with sensory processing disorders.

5. www.sensorystories.com
   This website links users to a web application of illustrated sensory e-stories for children with over-responsive sensory modulation.

6. www.SIFocus.com
   This is the website for *S.I. Focus*, the international magazine dedicated to improving sensory integration.

7. SPDconnection.com
   This is the website for Jenny's Kids Inc. founded by Jenny Clark Brack, OTR/L. The site is dedicated to providing sensory integration solutions for parents, teachers, and therapists. It lists activities, products and services.

8. www.SPDnetwork.org
   This is the website for The Sensory Processing Disorder Foundation. It is a project of the KID foundation, a nonprofit organization that focuses on research, education, and advocacy related to sensory processing disorders.

Recommended Children's Books

The following children's books are recommended as additional resources to explore and learn about kids with differing sensory processing patterns.

Berns, J. M., Chara, C. P., Chara, K. A., & Chara, P. J . (2004). *Sensory smarts: A book for kids with ADHD or autism spectrum disorders struggling with sensory integration problems*. London; Philadelphia: Jessica Kingsley Publishers.

Gagnon, E., & Myles, B. S. (1999). *This is Asperger Syndrome*. Shawnee Mission, KS: Autism Asperger Publishing Company.

Kranowitz, C. (2004). *The Goodenoughs get in sync: A story for kids*. Law Vegas, NV: Sensory Resources.

Larson, E. M. (2006). *I am utterly unique – Celebrating the strengths of children with Asperger Syndrome and high-functioning autism*. Shawnee Mission, KS: Autism Asperger Publishing Company.

Larson, E. M. (2007). *The kaleidoscope kid – Focusing on the strengths of children with Asperger Syndrome and high-functioning autism*. Shawnee Mission, KS: Autism Asperger Publishing Company.

Lowell, J., & Tuchel, T. (2005). *My best friend Will*. Shawnee Mission, KS: Autism Asperger Publishing Company.

Maguire, A. (2000). *Special people, special ways*. Arlington, TX: Future Horizons.

Murrell, D. (2004). *Oliver onion – The onion who learns to accept and be himself*. Shawnee Mission, KS: Autism Asperger Publishing Company.

Peralta, S. (2002). *All about my brother*. Shawnee Mission, KS: Autism Asperger Publishing Company

Renke, L. (2005). *I like birthdays ... it's the parties I'm not sure about*. Las Vegas, NV: Sensory Resources.

Autism Asperger Publishing Co.
P.O. Box 23173
Shawnee Mission, Kansas 66283-0173
www.asperger.net • 913-897-1004